Chloe's Secret Princess Club

Emma Barnes

Illustrated by Monique Dong

■SCHOLASTIC

♥ Chapter One ♥

If you want to know about our Secret Princess Club, it all started one morning during Mental Maths. Mental Maths is *really* boring. I often find myself drifting off.

For instance, last week our teacher, Mr Carter, read out the first question and I wrote down the answer straight away. (It was twenty-five.) Then I got the second answer, and the third. This had never happened before! I was so pleased I started imagining what would happen if I got every question right and came top of the class. Mr Carter would be amazed. Arthur, my twin, would be jealous. Our head teacher, Mrs Khan, would give me a Good Work certificate in Assembly ... maybe I would even turn out to be a child genius! The trouble is, I was so busy imagining that I forgot to listen to any more questions.

And I came bottom of the class.

That kind of thing happens to me a lot. My mum says it's because I've got so much imagination. My dad just calls me Chloe-in-the-clouds because he says my head is always in the clouds.

So this time, I tried to pay attention. I really did. Only I couldn't stop my eyes wandering about the room, and I saw that the door to the big cupboard-storeroom at the back of our classroom was open a tiny bit. Usually, that door is tight shut. In fact, Mr Carter keeps it locked. So I wondered why it wasn't today.

There must be a reason, I thought. And then my imagination began to whirr...

Maybe the reason that door was open was because it was a Portal to Another World!

If I went inside, who knew what might happen? After all, Lucy got into Narnia by going into a wardrobe in *The Lion, the*

Witch and the Wardrobe. So why not Chloe Higgins of Class 5C?

I was so busy dreaming that I didn't notice Mental Maths had finished and everyone else was handing in their answers. I didn't notice Mr Carter telling everyone to get ready for lunch. Or the lunch bell ringing. Or everyone lining up at the door.

"Chloe," Mr Carter called. "Stop dreaming and get moving!"

I almost jumped out of my skin.

Mr Carter was looking impatient, and my best friend, Aisha, was beckoning me, and Arthur and his friends were laughing at me.

I got up and scuttled towards the end of the line. And then ... I didn't mean to do it. *Really* I didn't. But somehow, while everyone else was filing out of the classroom, I couldn't help taking another quick peek towards the storeroom…

… and the next thing I knew, I'd stepped inside.

You see, it's not every day you have the chance to explore a Portal to Another World.

Only … it wasn't another world. It was just a big storeroom-cupboard. A musty-smelling place full of books and paint boxes and ukulele cases and boxes of costumes from school plays.

It was a bit disappointing, because I'd been hoping to go to Narnia and become a queen, the way Lucy did. Oh well.

I turned to open the door. But I couldn't. I'd shut the door behind me. And when it shut − it had locked.

Oh no! I tried again. I banged at the door and shouted, "Help!" Everybody had gone to lunch, though, and nobody heard me.

Oops.

Luckily it wasn't dark because there was a little window high up on one wall. But I still didn't like being shut in.

For a moment I felt scared. To distract myself, I looked at the school play costumes. There were lots for fairy tale characters, and I've always loved fairy tales. I put on a long, yellow wig, a blue dress and a golden crown.

First I pretended I was Lucy when she was Queen of Narnia, and then I imagined I was Cinderella, going to the ball.

Only then my stomach started rumbling. I wanted my lunch! That's when I had an idea. If I piled up all the ukulele cases, I could climb on top of them and reach the little window that looks out on to the playground. I could shout for help again.

It worked! The cases wobbled a bit, but I didn't fall off. I opened the window and leaned out.

"Help!" I squeaked.

The first person to notice me was Rachel, from my class. She was standing close by with some of her friends. It wasn't very nice of them to start giggling. Or to point at me so that other people started pointing and giggling too, until it seemed as if the whole playground was staring at me, Chloe Higgins.

That included Arthur and Mikhail and Barney, who had stopped playing football. And all the kids coming out of the dinner hall (including Aisha). And Mr Carter, who was on playground duty. And Mrs Khan, who was *clip-clopping* along on her high-heeled shoes with a clipboard under her arm.

"Who's that?"

"What's she doing?"

"Why's she up there?"

Even Mr Carter looked puzzled, as if he were wondering who I was.

"It's *Chloe*!" yelled Aisha suddenly. And Arthur said, "Yeah, you're right. What are you doing, Chlo?"

Then somebody (I think it was Barney) shouted, "It's not Chloe, it's *Rapunzel*!"

Everyone screamed with laughter.

"*Rapunzel, Rapunzel*," Barney shouted, "*let down your hair!*"

That's when I realized I was still wearing the long, blonde wig from the costumes box. And the crown. And the ball dress. And that, leaning out of the high window, I must have looked just like Rapunzel.

I could feel my face going beetroot red.

I tried to pull my head back out of the window so I could take off the wig. But I couldn't.

You see, it was a very small window. And

when I'd stuck my head into it – well, it got stuck.

It was the most embarrassing moment of my life. Even more embarrassing than the time I dropped my plate of school dinner on Mrs Khan's foot. (That's why I switched to packed lunches.) Or when I tucked my skirt into the back of my pants and didn't realize (until Barney Big Mouth pointed it out to everyone in Assembly).

Because not only was I wearing a wig. Not only was I locked in a storeroom. But now my head was stuck in a window, and maybe I was going to be looking out at the playground forever!

♥ Chapter Two ♥

At teatime, I kept making faces at Arthur. Faces that meant *Don't-Tell-Mum-And-Dad-About-Me-Getting-Stuck-In-A-Window*. You'd think he'd have understood. I mean, he's my twin. He was born the exact same hour as me. He's seen me practically every single day of his life.

Some people think twins have telepathy (that means they can read each other's thoughts). And, actually, I *can* read Arthur's thoughts. I know that most of the time he's thinking about football, and if he isn't then he's thinking about computer games, eating, or his pet rat, Haggis.

But Arthur definitely can't read my thoughts.

"Why are you making faces?" he asked me.

"I'm not making faces."

"You are so."

Dad had been too busy gobbling spaghetti to pay attention. Now he turned to me and Arthur and asked,

"How was school, you two? How was Mental Maths? It *was* Mental Maths today, right?"

I pretended my mouth was too full of spaghetti to answer.

"I got nineteen out of twenty," said Arthur.

"Well done! What about you, Chloe?"

"Um ... I think it was three out of twenty, or it might have been two, I can't remember. Maybe it was two and a half."

Dad groaned a *How-Does-She-Do-It* groan.

Mum said, "Chloe, were you dreaming again? Was Mr Carter cross? Arthur, was Mr Carter cross?"

"I don't think he was that cross ... considering."

"Considering what?" asked Mum.

"Considering what Chloe did."

"Arthur!" I shouted.

"What?"

"*I don't want them to know!*"

"Well, why didn't you say so?"

"Why d'you think I've been making faces at you?"

"I did wonder why you were doing that," said Arthur.

13

Then it all came out, including how Mrs Jenson the dinner lady had used butter to get my head free, and Mr Carter had said, "You are a dreamyhead, Chloe," and Mrs Khan had told me that she was very disappointed in me, and I must learn to act my age and be responsible.

"But why did you go into the cupboard?" asked Mum.

"I just thought that door must be open for a *reason*."

"And was it?"

"Yes. Mr Carter forgot to shut it."

Mum and Dad thought that was funny, but then they started going on and on about how I must learn to pay attention and stop dreaming and not lock myself into cupboards. I soon stopped listening and started wondering whether fairy tale princesses, like Rapunzel, ever ate spaghetti.

I couldn't really picture a princess eating spaghetti, as it's so hard to eat politely. Still, if I were a princess I wouldn't give it up. I'd eat it every single day.

"... and after all, Chloe, you can be anything you want to be if you believe in it and work hard," Mum was saying.

I stopped dreaming and gazed at Mum in amazement. "Really?"

"Of course," said Mum.

"I can really be a princess?"

They all stared at me. Arthur almost choked on his spaghetti.

"I meant," said Mum, "that you can be good at Mental Maths. But," she added, "if you want to be a princess, of course you can do that too."

This time, Dad and Arthur stared at *her*.

"No, she can't," said Dad.

"Not unless she marries a prince," said Arthur. "And she's too young. Besides, who'd marry Chloe?"

"She can be a princess in her heart," said Mum. Her eyes got a bit dreamy. "Even if Chloe gets carried away sometimes, a bit of imagination is a wonderful thing. And if you want something enough – and believe in it enough – who knows what might happen?"

"Oh, yes!" I whispered.

Arthur gave a rude snort.

Dad patted Mum's shoulder. "Sometimes," he said, "I can see where Chloe gets it from." Then he got up and made for the door.

"Where are you going?" Mum asked. "It's your turn to clear the table."

Dad paused in the doorway, and made a sweeping gesture with his arm. "Tonight," he announced grandly, "I want to be a king! So I'm going to believe I'm a king and act like a king. And kings never, ever clear tables!"

That evening I wanted to watch TV, but Mum had other ideas.

"Your room really does need tidying, Chloe," she said, walking me into my bedroom.

"It looks fine," I protested.

"Then why," asked Mum quietly, "are you standing in a bowl of cornflakes?"

"Oh," I said, hopping on one foot. "I was wondering what that soggy feeling was."

Mum went off to find Arthur, and make him tidy his room too. I looked round. It was a bit of a mess. Well, quite a lot of a mess. Well, actually a *huge* mess.

I pulled off my squelchy sock and spread

it out to dry on Hammy's cage. "I know just how Cinderella felt," I told him, "when she was made to slave and skivvy for her cruel stepmother." But that gave me an idea. I could pretend I was Cinderella! That way tidying up might even be fun.

I sang a special "Tidy Up" song as I put things away.

There was so much stuff. I found Dad's cufflinks that he'd been searching for the time we went to Auntie Jackie's wedding. (Oops.)

And the library book that we couldn't find so we had to pay for a new copy. (Oops again.)

And my old hobby horse, Dobbin, wedged down the side of the wardrobe. I'd been wondering where he was. I gave him a kiss on the nose.

When I'd finished, you could see the

floor again. You could even see the mirror on my dressing table. I stared into it.

"*Mirror, mirror on the wall*
Who is the fairest of them all?"

Probably not Chloe. Not with the smudge on my nose. Or all those freckles. And yes … that *was* a piece of spaghetti stuck to my hair.

Still, Mum had said I really *could* be a princess if I wanted. Me, ordinary, head-in-the-clouds Chloe.

Of course, I might have to work at it a bit.

Mum put her head round the door. "That's looking a lot better, Chloe," she said. She sounded surprised. "Well done."

"Would you say it was fit for a princess?"

"Well … there's a bit of a pong."

She was right. A princess's room does not smell of hamster.

So I cleaned out Hammy's cage. Afterwards I was really tired. I stopped being Cinderella and imagined I was Sleeping Beauty instead.

I lay on my newly-made bed and I let Hammy sit on my tummy while I talked to him. Sometimes I wish I'd chosen a rat, not a hamster, because to be honest, Haggis, Arthur's rat, is a lot more interesting than Hammy. Hammy sleeps all day, and then wakes me up in the middle of the night, running on his wheel.

On the other hand, Hammy is very good-tempered when I wake *him* up in what must be the middle of the night for *him*. If *I* were a hamster and somebody picked *me* up from my warm, cosy bed, I'd probably bite them. Also, he is cute.

He was sitting washing his fur.

"Hammy," I said, "you've got to improve your act. No more chucking food out of your cage. You are the hamster of a princess."

Hammy nibbled one of his paws.

"We are going to do all kinds of exciting things," I told him. "I'm not quite sure what yet, but princess-y things. You'll see."

And then I looked round my room again. I had to admit that even now it was tidy, it still didn't look fit for a princess.

A princess, I thought, would have blue walls, pale as a summer sky, with silver stars all over them. A princess would have a soft, white rug made of swan's feathers. A princess would have a four-poster bed.

A princess would *not* have ripped wallpaper where a hamster had been chewing at it. Or Blu-tack stuck to the carpet. Or curtains with pictures of Paddington Bear.

I had an idea. I jumped up and grabbed Dobbin. We went galloping on to the landing.

"Mum," I yelled. "I need to ask you something *now*!"

It was bad luck that Mum was coming up the stairs at that moment. And that Arthur was coming out of his bedroom with his arms full of used bedding from Haggis's cage.

CRASH!

Smelly hay and rat droppings went all over Mum.

Mum doesn't get mad much, but this time she was so cross she looked like a fire-breathing dragon, except that fire-breathing dragons don't have hay all over their heads.

She said, "Clear it all up THIS MINUTE!"

It didn't seem the best moment to tell her my idea about getting a four-poster bed.

Chapter Three

I was hoping that everyone at school would have forgotten about me getting stuck in the window. They hadn't. The next day, at break, they all came crowding round.

"Oh, Chloe, you did look funny," giggled Georgia. Georgia is a giggler.

"Rapunzel, Rapunzel, let down your hair!" squeaked Keira, dancing around in circles. Keira is a show-off.

"Chloe got stuck in the window – the

24

window – the window!" yelled Barney Big Mouth.

Luckily the boys soon got bored and went off to play football, but the girls hung about.

"Why were you pretending to be Rapunzel anyway?" asked Rachel in a grown-up sounding voice.

Rachel is one of those people who never do anything silly. I bet she didn't even wet her nappy when she was a baby. She is always coming top in things, and being given certificates in Assembly by Mrs Khan.

"I suppose you never make mistakes, Rachel!" said Aisha. It was nice of her to defend me, because Aisha is quite shy.

"I'd certainly never lock myself in a cupboard," said Rachel in a snooty voice. "Or play pretend games."

"I wasn't playing pretend games!" I said.

"Yes, you were. You were *pretending* to be Rapunzel."

"I wasn't!"

"Rapunzel, Rapunzel!" shrieked Keira again, and Georgia giggled so much I thought she was going to explode.

"Do be quiet, you two," said Eliza fiercely. Eliza is the fiercest girl in our class. She sounds fierce even when she says, "Pass me a pencil." She turned to me. "*Were* you pretending or weren't you?"

"I wasn't pretending," I said.

"But you must have been," said Rachel.

"I was being Princess Chloe."

"Then you *were* playing pretend games."

"No, I wasn't! I wasn't pretending because I *am* a princess."

They all stared at me. Then all of them, except for Eliza and Aisha, began to laugh.

"Chloe thinks she's a princess!"

26

"Yes, she does!"

"Princess Chloe!"

Aisha nudged me. "Chloe," she whispered. "You know you're not really a princess!"

"I am so! You see, my mum says you can be anything if you really believe in it, even if you're not, and that imagination is a good thing, except for Mental Maths, and that's why we can all be a princess if we want."

They were just staring at me like I was crazy. Somehow, it had sounded better when my mum said it.

I had an idea. "It's like this film I watched once. It's called *A Little Princess*. The girl in that – she's called Sara – *she* wasn't a real princess either. She didn't have a crown or a throne or a kingdom. But because she had a wonderful imagination, and she *believed* she was a princess, then somehow that's what she was. She behaved like a princess and everybody treated her like one. So, you see, we can be princesses too."

There was a pause.

Rachel sniffed. "It all sounds a bit silly to me. Anyway, Sports Leaders' Club is starting." And they all went off to the other side of the playground to join in with the sprints and star jumps.

Aisha and I drifted in the other direction. Aisha was looking thoughtful.

"Do you really think we can be princesses, Chloe? Really and truly?"

"Of course I do!"

"I would love to but…"

"But what?"

"I live in an ordinary house with three little brothers making a mess everywhere. I can't be a princess. I'm … I'm not special enough."

"Yes you are!" I thought hard. "I mean you have the best handwriting in the whole class, Mr Carter says! And you have the longest eyelashes!"

Aisha was pleased. "Do you think so?"

"Definitely. Only a princess would have eyelashes that long."

Aisha clasped her hands. "I'd love to live in a palace. And to have my own unicorn. A princess could have a pet unicorn, couldn't they?"

Before I could reply, there was a cough behind us. I turned and saw Eliza.

"Are you serious about this princess business, Chloe?" she asked.

"Yes," I said firmly. "I am. And Rachel and that lot can think what they like!"

Eliza nodded. "In that case, *I'd* like to be a princess too."

We gazed at her in astonishment. I don't

know Eliza very well. I've been to her house a few times. But I don't know her well enough to share secrets, or play pretend games with her, like Aisha and I do. (We *do* play pretend games sometimes, even though I told Rachel we didn't.)

She was the last person I'd ever have thought would want to be a princess.

"Why do you want to?" I asked.

Eliza went red. "I just do."

"Then let's do it!" I said. "After all, you can do anything if you believe in it and work hard!"

"I'm happy to work hard," said Eliza.

"Me too," said Aisha.

My imagination was fizzing. "We'll form a club. The Princess Club."

"Oh, yes!" said Aisha.

"The *Secret* Princess Club," said Eliza. "So that Rachel and the others don't know."

"Definitely secret," I agreed. "*Top* secret!"
We looked at each other and beamed.
"This is going to be *fun*," said Aisha.
And that's how the Secret Princess Club
began.

Chapter Four

It was very important that we got together as soon as possible to decide about our Secret Princess Club.

"Somewhere private," I whispered, as we lined up to go inside after break.

"Not school," Aisha agreed.

"After school, then," said Eliza. "At my house."

We tried to pick a day. It wasn't easy.

Aisha (who is Muslim) goes to classes

at her mosque most days after school. And on Wednesdays she plays netball.

Eliza (who is Jewish) has Friday Night Dinner with her family every Friday.

"And," she said, "on Mondays I have trumpet lessons, on Tuesdays tap dancing, on Thursdays it's karate, on Fridays..."

It made Aisha and me exhausted just hearing about all the things Eliza did.

"It used to be worse," said Eliza. "At least Mum's let me give up yoga."

As for me, I'm not that busy, but Arthur and I go swimming on Tuesdays, and I go to Baking Club on Wednesdays.

After a lot of discussion, we thought we'd ask our mums if we could meet on Wednesday, after Aisha and I had finished netball and baking. This would, Eliza said, also give her time to practise her trumpet before we got there.

★

"I hope Eliza's not going to try and run everything," whispered Aisha, as we waited with my mum at Eliza's front door.

"If she does, we'll just stand up to her," I whispered back. "Even if she does know karate!" Aisha giggled.

Mum had been a bit surprised when I'd asked to go to Eliza's house. She knew we weren't close friends. And of course I couldn't explain about the new Princess Club. It was secret from everyone! But she'd agreed, and she stopped to chat to Eliza's mum while Aisha and I followed Eliza upstairs. As soon as we arrived in her bedroom, Eliza sat herself on the best beanbag. "Let's get to it," she said, opening the cover of a notebook and picking up a pen. "How's this Princess Club going to work?"

"Actually, I think Chloe's the one who should write things down," said Aisha. "After all, it was her idea."

"But it's *my* room," Eliza pointed out. "And my notebook." It was a very pretty notebook with a unicorn on the cover.

Things can be tricky when there's three of you. With Aisha and me, sometimes I'm the boss, and sometimes she is, and though we do argue, because we have been best friends forever we are used to taking turns.

"Maybe Aisha should take notes," I said. "She's best at writing."

"Actually, Mr Carter said my last piece of writing was exceptional," said Eliza. "He said I put the case for better school dinners very persuasively."

"Yes," I said, "and he also said he could hardly read it, it was so messy."

Eliza loves using long words. But she didn't impress me.

"Hmmmm," said Eliza. She handed the notebook and pen to Aisha, though.

"Right," said Aisha. "I'll take notes. And I'll look after the notebook. But I still think Chloe should be the leader of the club. She has the best ideas."

Eliza frowned. "How do you know *I* won't have the best ideas?"

"Well," said Aisha. "Look at this room. It doesn't look like it belongs to the kind of person who wants to be a princess."

Eliza's room is high up in the attic. It has sloping ceilings, with windows that look out over rooftops. Eliza once saw an owl through her window. She's got a purple stripy duvet, and lots of cushions, and animal posters and a globe of the world and seventeen teddy bears. She even has her own bathroom. It's called an ensuite — which means you walk into it from her bedroom.

Aisha and I were very jealous of the bathroom. "No Arthur leaving his football kit on the floor," I said. "No Hari and Abdullah and Ibrahim sitting in the bath when I need to go," said Aisha. (Aisha has three little brothers.)

But Aisha was right. There wasn't anything princess-y.

"That's where you're wrong," Eliza said. She crawled under the bed and came out holding a shoebox. "Do you *promise* to keep a secret?"

"Of course," I said. "After all, it's Secret Club."

So Eliza took about fifteen rubber bands off the shoebox and showed us what was inside.

♥ *A peg doll wearing a silver doily dress and golden crown*
♥ *A sparkling bracelet of pink glass*
♥ *A matching sparkling earring (she'd lost the other one)*
♥ *Figurines of Elsa and Ana from Frozen*
♥ *Photos of ball dresses from magazines*
♥ *A pink silk rose*

"Ooh!" we said.

"Why do you keep it under the bed?"

Aisha asked, holding the rose against her hair.

"Mum doesn't approve," said Eliza. "She gets this look on her face." Eliza crinkled her nose like she had tasted something nasty.

"Do you mean she'd make you throw it out?"

"She'd be disappointed in me. You see, when *she* was little, *her* mum wanted her to be interested in pretty things, like party dresses and fairies. But she was only interested in sport and animals. So now she only wants me to like sports and serious things, like she did. Or homework. She'd think all this stuff was silly. That's why this secret club is perfect for me."

Aisha and I were silent. We were seeing a new side to Eliza.

"I'm glad you're in our club," said Aisha suddenly.

I nodded. "And we don't need a leader," I added. "We'll all run the club together."

Then Aisha gave a squeak. "I forgot. I made us these."

She took out three little badges from her pocket. They were purple with a P (for princess) written in silver, and a tiny crown over the P.

"They're gorgeous! I wish I could make things as well as you," I said, as I pinned one on.

For the next ten minutes we made lots of important decisions and Aisha wrote them down in the unicorn notebook.

The Secret Princess Club

Members:

Princess Clarinda (Chloe)

Princess Araminta (Aisha)

Princess Elisabetta (Eliza)

Motto: Act Like A Princess And
You Can Be A Princess

Rules:

The Princesses Must Stick
Up For Each Other.
The Princesses Must Call
Each Other by Their
Princess Names.
The Princess Club Is Secret.
<u>Nobody Must Know!!!</u>
Princesses Forever.

"Yes, but what are we going to *do*?" asked Eliza.

Luckily, I'd already been thinking about that. "Let's all write down what we think princesses do, and then we can read out our ideas and..."

"And what?" asked Eliza.

"Well, and then we choose the best of them, I guess."

"Yes!" Aisha was bouncing up and down with excitement. "We'll have a Princess Challenge! When we've managed to do enough things, we'll be really, truly princesses, and – and..."

"We'll have a party," Eliza suggested.

"A coronation!" I said.

We grinned at each other and then started writing down our ideas.

Aisha read out her list first.

Aisha's List

Wear a tiara
Be kind to the sick
Have perfect manners
Kiss a frog
Marry a prince

Eliza and I were very impressed. Although we did agree that it might be hard finding sick people for us to be kind to (Aisha suggested we could go to the nearest hospital, but I wasn't sure how they'd feel about three unknown princesses turning up at the door).

Eliza also said we didn't know any princes to get married to, and I said we weren't old enough, and anyway, I didn't want to get married to one, and Aisha said neither did she, really, it was just that we were listing what princesses did and marrying princes was something that they did. We agreed to leave that one out for the moment.

Then we read Eliza's list.

Eliza's List
Wear long dresses
Be a role model
World peace (we want it)
Always wear pink
Wave a lot

Again, we were impressed. Except I didn't want to wear pink ALL the time, and I also thought world peace might be tricky, though Eliza said there were lots of things we could do to help.

"Like what?" I asked.

"We can write to people," said Eliza. "Like queens and presidents and ... um ... people."

Aisha and I said that would be fine, just so long as Eliza did the writing.

Then it was my turn. I was afraid that after the others, it would sound a bit soppy.

Chloe's List
Make friends with unicorns
Rescue kittens
Have a lovely bedroom (with a four-poster bed)
Do things from fairy tales
Make princess food
Write poetry
Learn to dance (so that we can go to a ball)

Aisha and Eliza were actually really nice about my ideas. Although Eliza said it might be hard to find a unicorn. And Aisha said it was bad enough writing poems at school, and she didn't really see that it had anything to do with being a princess. (It doesn't – it's just that I like writing poems.)

It was harder to decide which ideas we should do first. We spent ages discussing it. Then we realized that we had completely forgotten to call each other by our princess names. And by then we felt a bit peckish, so we thought making princess cakes and sweets might be just the place to start.

We crept downstairs to the kitchen very, very quietly because we didn't want anyone interrupting us. There were loads of stairs because Eliza's house is very tall, and the kitchen is down in the basement, but luckily Eliza knows which stairs creak and could warn us in time.

"I feel just like Sleeping Beauty, creeping

out of the castle to get away from her wicked stepmother," I whispered.

"I don't think Sleeping Beauty *had* a wicked stepmother," Aisha replied.

"I mean Cinderella, then."

"But she didn't creep – she ran really fast because the clock chimed midnight."

"All right, I feel like Snow White."

"*She* was taken away from the castle by one of her stepmother's servants."

"Well, I'm sure there must have been *some* princess *some* time or other who had to creep out of a castle, and that's who I feel like right now."

"Shhhh!" said Eliza. "Here we are!"

We burst into the kitchen, ready to start cake-making, but that's when our plans went wrong. Eliza's mum was there, and when Eliza said we wanted to do some baking, she said, "Don't be silly, sweetie! You don't want horrible, sugary stuff that's bad for your teeth. I'll fix you all some lovely, healthy vegetables instead."

While we were reluctantly crunching carrots, I had a brilliant idea. "I know. We'll have a Princess Sleepover! We can do lots of baking then."

♥ Chapter Five ♥

"I can't wait until Saturday!" I said.

"Shhh!" Aisha hissed.

"I don't think anyone can hear."

It was Monday lunchtime and we were in Computer Club. Miss Hammond was in charge, as usual, but unless people get too noisy, or too silly, she doesn't interfere.

Eliza, Aisha and me were sitting around the same computer. We were looking up recipes for our sleepover. Everyone else was too busy playing games to notice us.

"Let's make these jam tarts," said Eliza hungrily.

"They look scrummy," Aisha said. "I can never make things like that without my brothers eating them all."

"We'd better not have the sleepover at yours, then," said Eliza. "What did your mum say when you asked, Chloe?"

"Weeellll…"

What Mum had actually said was, "*Must* you?" and, "Can't you wait until the holidays?" Dad had said, "Surely Chloe and Arthur make enough chaos between them without having a whole load of their friends here as well." But they'd agreed in the end.

"Or we could have it at mine," said Eliza, before I could finish. "That might be best. I have the biggest bedroom."

"Actually, Mum said it was fine," I said

quickly. I had caught Aisha's eye and I could tell we were thinking the same thing – we didn't want Eliza thinking she was the boss.

"But…"

"Anyway," Aisha interrupted, "Mum won't let me go to a sleepover unless it's at Chloe's."

"Why not?"

"Aisha's mum doesn't allow sleepovers," I told Eliza. "Not unless she knows the parents really well. She knows my mum really well because they met at a baby group when we were teeny-tiny."

Eliza looked like she was going to argue. Then she gave a huge grin. "You know what – I'd rather go to yours, Chloe. That way my mum can't make us eat vegetables all the time."

Suddenly we were all really excited about the Princess Sleepover. Aisha said she'd bring lots of her mum's headscarves for dressing up, and Eliza said she'd bring a big book of fairy tales. I typed out a list of things for Mum and Dad to get for baking.

Then we all linked little fingers and gave the secret princess finger shake that we'd invented. Up, down, up! We could hardly wait.

It seemed to take ages for the weekend to come, but when Saturday finally arrived I made a terrible discovery. Arthur was having Mikhail for a sleepover too!

"It's not fair," I grumbled to Dad, who was unpacking the supermarket shop.

"Life *is* unfair," said Dad, shoving cereal into a cupboard.

"And another thing," I said. "Who will get the telly? We've got a film we want to watch after tea, and I don't think they'll want to watch the same one." (As it was *A Little Princess*, I was almost certain they wouldn't.)

"That reminds me," said Dad. "I got this for you in the supermarket."

He handed me a DVD called *Ballroom Magic – Learn At Home!*

"Ooh, thanks, Dad. Aisha and Eliza will love this! Of course," I added, "ballroom dancing *lessons* would be even better."

"No lessons, Chloe," said Dad firmly.

"Why not?"

"You *know* why not. Because you begged and begged to do ballet, and we paid for that, and you went off it. Then you wanted to do tap dancing, so we paid for that, and then you went off it. And then you wanted…"

"This is *completely* different!"

"How?"

"Because I might need to go to a ball!"

Dad just laughed. And of course I couldn't explain about the Secret Princess Club.

Soon after that, Eliza and Aisha arrived. We did our special Princess Finger Shake, and checked we were wearing our Princess Badges, then got down to business.

"We need to do something for our Princess Challenge," I said. "Something from our lists."

"Baking!" said Eliza.

"Dancing!" said Aisha.

We decided to bake first. We made strawberry, blackcurrant and apricot tarts. Yum.

"Chloe, you have jam all round your mouth," said Eliza. "You're supposed to be putting it in the tarts, not eating it."

"You mean *Princess Clarinda*," Aisha reminded her. She looked at me and giggled. "There's some on your nose too."

"Who cares?" I said cheerfully. "You have to test the ingredients when you're baking!"

We got Dad to put the tarts in the oven, and then it was time for the ballroom dancing.

We arrived in the living room at exactly the same moment as Arthur and Mikhail, and raced each other to get to the DVD player.

"We were here first!" Arthur panted. "We want to watch our dinosaur film."

"Well, bad luck, we're doing ballroom dancing!"

"Ballroom dancing! Yuk!"

"Stupid old dinosaurs!"

In the end, we won, probably because there were three of us, and Eliza is very fierce *and* does karate, and as Arthur said to Mikhail, if they had a big fight with us now, the sleepover might be called off. They went off upstairs instead.

We put the DVD into the machine. A lady in a gorgeous red dress appeared on the screen, along with a tall man wearing a shiny suit and a bow tie. "Now you are going to learn ballroom dancing," the lady announced. "Just get ready to copy us." And they started twirling around a huge hall.

"Hey, how are we going to do this?" asked Eliza. "We need to dance in pairs."

"We'll just have to take turns," I said. So two of us danced together, while one of us bobbed and twirled by themselves.

It wasn't as easy as it looked.

"You're treading on me!"

"You're going the wrong way!"

"Stop banging into me, you two," I said, backing into the coffee table and sending everything crashing to the floor.

"Let's start again," Aisha said, helping me pick up the remote controls and Mum's knitting from the floor. "And let's all take teeny-tiny steps. I expect that's what princesses do. Anyway, we don't have as

much room as they do on the DVD."

We all took teeny-tiny steps.

We were doing quite well, I thought, until Eliza suddenly waved to us to be still.

"What is it?"

She pointed at the door, and then I heard it too – muttering and giggling.

We looked at each other. Eliza crept towards the door...

Chapter Six

Eliza pulled the door open very quickly and Arthur and Mikhail almost fell into the room. They were snorting with laughter.

"You were spying on us!" I accused them.

"You sneaky sneaks!" said Eliza.

"You looked like a load of wallies," said Mikhail. And he began to wobble around the room, pretending to be us dancing.

Eliza and me were ready for a fight, but Aisha was cleverer than that.

"Oh, Mikhail! I didn't know you liked dancing!" She grabbed hold of him and began to waltz him around the room. Eliza and me grinned at the look of horror on his face.

"Lemme go!" Mikhail yelled, and he and Arthur ran for it, while we three princesses collapsed into giggles. After we stopped laughing, we decided we'd done enough dancing for the moment. We went up to my room.

I felt a bit embarrassed by how scruffy it looked. "I know it's not as nice as yours," I told Eliza, who had rushed over to take a look at Hammy. "I keep saying I *need* a four-poster bed, but Mum and Dad just won't agree."

"Never mind," said Aisha.

"Let's build a Princess Boo-doo-wah," said Eliza.

"A *what*?" I said.

"A *boo-doo-wah*. It's a kind of princess den."

We made Eliza write it down, and it was actually spelled BOUDOIR and apparently it was the kind of lovely place a princess would hang out in, with flowers and silk curtains. So after a bit of tidying, we did our best to make one next to my wardrobe.

We picked flowers from the garden, and put them in Mum's best crystal vase. We borrowed some of her candlesticks too. We took Aisha's mum's headscarves and tied them to some of my mum's beanpoles, to make a kind of canopy. It looked really lovely, until Aisha tried to crawl inside — and it collapsed on her head!

"Never mind, let's dress up as princesses instead," said Eliza.

We rummaged about in my dressing-up

box, but there weren't enough things, so I decided to look in Mum's wardrobe.

"You don't think she'll mind, do you?" asked Aisha anxiously.

"Oh no," I said airily, as I held up a shawl printed with pink roses. "She never uses any of this stuff."

I wore a blue dress with sequins and one of Mum's necklaces.

Eliza wore a floaty pink petticoat, the shawl and my old ballet shoes.

Aisha wore a wonderful oriental-looking dressing gown with a red silk scarf as a sash.

Then we all bounced on my bed. We kept tripping over our long skirts but that just made us giggle harder.

"We are the incredible trampolining princesses!" I yelled, as we collapsed in a heap.

When we'd recovered, Eliza said, "What

fairy tale thing shall we do now?" and Aisha said, "Do you remember *The Princess and the Pea*?"

That immediately got Eliza and me interested. We looked in Eliza's book and read again the story of how there was a princess who couldn't sleep a wink because there was a pea under her pile of mattresses, and that's how everyone knew she was a "real" princess.

"Shall we see if we can feel a pea?" Aisha suggested. I ran downstairs and found a packet of frozen peas in the freezer and sneaked them upstairs. After a lot of tugging, we managed to get my mattress off the bed.

But when I put one tiny pea on the wooden base, it looked very sad and small.

"I'm sure that can't be what the story meant," said Eliza. "Put on a few more."

"*Of course* that was what it meant," said

63

Aisha. "It was because it was so small that only a princess could feel it."

"Well, I think that pea will just get squashed, or melt or something."

Then I had a brilliant idea.

"Let's act it out. As if it were real. *The Princess and the Pea*. It will be *much* more fun that way!"

Eliza and Aisha agreed at once. We all wanted to be the princess in the story, but eventually we decided I could, because it was my house, and that Eliza would be the queen and Aisha the prince. ("But I'm being the princess next time," said Aisha firmly, "because I got the worst part this time.")

I went and wrapped myself in Dad's grey bathrobe to look like I was wearing a cloak against the storm, and wet my hair under the shower so that it would look like I was drenched by the rain. I could hear Aisha in my bedroom saying to Eliza, "Oh, dearest mother, where will I ever find a *real* princess!"

I knocked on my bedroom door.

"Oh, please can I have a shelter for the night?" I begged, when Eliza opened the door, looking very proud and queenly.

"Who are you, my child?" she replied.

"I am Princess Clarinda, caught in a terrible storm, and I need a place to stay!"

"Come in," said Eliza graciously.

So I went into my bedroom, and Aisha (the prince) took my cloak (bathrobe) and hung it over a chair.

"Hey, you've done a great job on the bed," I said, catching sight of it.

"Shhhh," hissed Aisha. "You're not supposed to know!"

"Sorry," I whispered.

While I'd been fetching the bathrobe and wetting my hair, Eliza and Aisha had piled loads of mattresses on my bed, just like in the story. Well, they weren't really mattresses, but there were two camping mats, the duvet from the spare room, a travel rug, and a big cloak from my dressing-up box.

"Oh, Handsome Prince and Noble Queen," I continued more loudly, "may I go to sleep now, on this wonderful bed? For I am footsore and weary after my travels through the storm. Also, I'm tired," I added, just in case they hadn't got the message.

Aisha bowed. "Goodnight and sweet dreams."

I climbed on to the bed, while Eliza said, "Sleep well, dearest Princess Clarinda – on these pillows of soft goose down…"

And that's when we heard it – a sniggering

noise, from behind the door. Arthur and Mikhail were eavesdropping *again*.

We were furious. We grabbed the pillows and rushed on to the landing.

They were almost crying with laughter. "Oh, Princess Pretty-Pops," squeaked Arthur in a high voice that didn't sound anything like us. "Oh, Royal Prince Stinky-Socks!" gasped Mikhail, leaning against the banisters.

We bashed them over the head with pillows. They were giggling so much they found it hard to fight back, and we were really enjoying ourselves and definitely winning until…

"CHLOE!"

It was Dad shouting from downstairs. We'd forgotten all about our jam tarts, and they had burned to a crisp.

Oops!

Chapter Seven

Dad made sausages and chips for tea. Eliza and Aisha had vegetarian ones because they don't eat pork, and I did, too, to keep them company.

We also had green beans. "Yuk. Why can't we have peas?" complained Arthur.

"Because there aren't any," said Dad. "Which is strange, because I was sure there was a packet in the freezer."

Eliza and Aisha and I tried not to catch one another's eyes.

While we ate, we argued with the boys, who kept making silly jokes.

"Why are you wearing those clothes?" asked Arthur. "What are you supposed to be?"

"We're practising for the school play," I said, which I thought was quite clever, except that unfortunately Aisha said at the same moment, "We're making a film for YouTube."

Arthur looked suspicious. "What school play?"

"It's a secret," I said. "Only Mr Carter knows about it."

"And we're going to film it and put it on YouTube," added Aisha.

"What have *you* been doing?" asked Eliza. "Besides spying on us?"

71

"Oh, we're being detectives," said Arthur. I didn't like the sound of that. I didn't want them doing any detecting and working out about our Secret Princess Club. I glared at him, but he just waggled his eyebrows at me.

There was chocolate cake and ice cream for dessert. Eliza really enjoyed it. "This is *so much* nicer than healthy fruit!" she declared, as she took her third helping.

After tea, we all wanted to watch a film, so Dad tossed a coin and the boys won. "What shall we do?" I asked.

"Let's go and play with Hammy," said Eliza.

"Why don't we build him his own royal palace out of a cardboard box?" Aisha suggested.

We all loved that idea. On the way to my bedroom, we stopped next to the living room door. "What are the boys doing?" Eliza wondered. "All those banging noises?"

THUMP! CLUMP! BUMP!

"They're *meant* to be watching a film," I said doubtfully, "but they sound like ... like a buffalo stampede!"

"That's boys for you," said Aisha gloomily. "You wouldn't believe how much noise my brothers make. Sometimes the whole house shakes!"

It was bad luck that at that moment Mum came back from her friend's house. The first thing she saw was the three of us, wearing her things, and she wasn't pleased.

"Chloe, what *are* you wearing ... *not* my best dress ... and that is my *favourite* shawl that I bought for Aunt Jackie's wedding..."

"I thought they were things you didn't wear any more," I said in a small voice.

"No, they're things I don't wear *very often* – but that's because I keep them for Special Occasions."

Oops.

We went upstairs to take them off. And that's when Mum caught sight of our Princess Boudoir, with her favourite crystal vase and the roses we'd picked from her flowerbeds, and her beanpoles and her candlesticks. And she wasn't very pleased about that, either.

She didn't say much because my friends were there but her eyes went all cross and glinty and she made us take down the boudoir.

After she'd left, I sat on the floor feeling really sorry for myself.

"Oh, dear," I said, sniffing sadly. "Everything's spoiled."

"But it's a lovely sleepover." Aisha handed

me one of her special pink tissues so I could dab my eyes, which were a bit wet.

"Yes, we'd never have had chocolate cake at our house," Eliza agreed. "Or jam tarts. Even burned ones."

"And your mum wasn't *that* cross," Aisha said. "My mum would have been crosser."

"Mine too," Eliza agreed.

Aisha hugged me, and Eliza fetched Hammy so he could nuzzle my cheek. Then Aisha fetched the unicorn notebook from her backpack so we could write down all the things we had done.

<u>Princess Challenges</u>
Baking jam tarts ✓
Learning to ballroom dance
(well, made a start) 1/2
Making a Princess Boudoir
(until it broke) 1/2

Aisha pointed out that we hadn't finished Hammy's palace yet. So we got to work. I fetched lots of things from the recycling and Eliza made the battlements from egg boxes while I made the turrets from toilet rolls. Aisha did the decorations, because she is so good at art. She drew roses growing on the walls, and used silver foil to make the roof shiny, and she pinned a tiny flag with the special "princess" P on one of the turrets.

We let Hammy explore his new home and he really enjoyed running around the battlements and up and down the kitchen roll that we had turned into the grand stairway!

After that, we were really tired. We climbed into our pyjamas, and just then Mum came in with mugs of cocoa with marshmallows on top. She gave me a quick kiss on my head before she went out, so I knew she wasn't mad at me any more.

The cocoa was lovely. Aisha couldn't manage all of hers, so Eliza finished it for her.

Then we crawled into my bed.

"I'm so tired I can't move!"

"Me too, Elisabetta."

"Move over, Araminta."

"I'll fall out if I do, Clarinda!"

"Sleep tight, everyone."

"Sleep tight."

I was drifting off to sleep when Aisha whispered, "My toes feel damp."

"Mine too," Eliza agreed.

At that moment, my toes felt the wet bit.

"Has somebody had an accident?" I whispered. "It's OK to say if you have."

"No!" squeaked Aisha.

"No!" squeaked Eliza. And they looked at me accusingly.

"Hey, it wasn't me either!" I threw back the duvet cover. And there, right in the middle of the bed, was the packet of frozen peas! They had melted all over the sheet.

We started giggling.

"It's been a wonderful evening," whispered Aisha sleepily as we settled down again. "The Secret Princess Club was a really good idea. Don't you think so, Elisabetta?"

But Eliza didn't answer. She was snoring!

♥ Chapter Eight ♥

It's hard work being a princess, I can tell you.

For the next week, we practised all of our Princess Tasks.

We did lots of waving until we got really good and hardly ever hit each other in the face by mistake.

We could curtsey without wobbling most of the time. (Of course, as Eliza said, really other people should curtsey to *us*, but it was a bit difficult to tell them that, given that our Princess Club is Top Secret.)

We helped the sick. Well, we gave soup to the little old lady who lives next door to Aisha and who has a bad foot, though she didn't seem very pleased. I think maybe our soup was a bit lumpy.

We even rescued a kitten. It was quite a *big* kitten, actually my mum said it was more or less a full-grown cat, and she was quite grumpy about helping us find its owner, especially when the cat turned

out to live next door but one and wasn't even lost.

And we made our own tiaras. They were beautiful. Or they were until mine fell off when I was practising ballroom dancing and I trod on it and it broke.

"It's not always easy, being a princess," I told Eliza one lunchtime. We had finished our packed lunches and were sitting in the playground, waiting for Aisha.

"Shhh!" said Eliza, looking towards Rachel who was doing Sports Leaders' Club.

"Nobody can hear us."

It was true. Rachel and her friends were too busy doing star jumps with Mr Carter, and Arthur and his friends were playing football.

"Have your mum and dad changed their mind about dance classes?" Eliza asked.

"No. They won't buy me a ball dress either."

"Me neither." Eliza sighed. "My parents don't understand the needs of a princess. Mum got cross with me yesterday for putting glitter in my hair."

"Dad got cross with *me* because he sat on my tiara. The broken one. I guess it was a bit spiky in the bottom area!"

We giggled.

"But I'll never be able to mend it now," I added sadly. "It is a hundred per cent squashed."

"I expect a lot of princesses have rotten parents," said Eliza.

"Most of them do, if you think about fairy tales."

I scratched a scab on my knee. That's another thing. In fairy tales, princesses might have to sleep in the cinders and scrub

83

floors for their wicked stepmothers. But do they ever get scabs that fall off and bleed all over their clean white socks?

Aisha flopped down beside us. "It was Quorn bake *again*," she told us gloomily. "And they ran out of chips."

"Cheer up," I said. "Do you know what we need? An exciting new Princess Challenge!"

We looked at each other. Nobody could think of anything.

"We've *done* everything," said Aisha.

"We *can't* have," said Eliza.

"WE NEED a little magic, that's what we need," I said. "That will get us going again."

Eliza snorted. "Magic! Are you kidding?"

Aisha wasn't listening. "What's going on there?" She pointed at Barney and Mikhail near the fence.

"Oh, probably nothing," I said. "Just a squashed beetle. Or an apple core. Or something even yukkier. You know what boys are like."

"I'm going to see," said Eliza.

"She's probably going to boss them," Aisha whispered, as we went after her.

She was.

"You leave the poor little thing alone," she was saying. "How do you think poking it with that stick is going to help?"

"I'm just seeing if it's alive," said Barney.

"You can tell it's alive because it's breathing, but if you keep doing that it'll probably have a heart attack and die!"

Aisha and I bent to look.

"It's a frog," I said. "Or is it a toad?"

"It's a frog," said Eliza firmly. "Poor little thing!" And she glared at Barney and Mikhail.

I crouched down. The frog was sitting

very still, but I could see that it was breathing, because its skin was moving.

"You silly thing," I said softly. "You'll get trodden on if you stay there."

"We saw it first," said Mikhail.

"So?" said Aisha.

"So it's ours."

"No it isn't," said Eliza. "*You* are not responsible frog carers."

"We are so!"

He shouted so loudly that Mr Carter heard. "Hey, what's going on over there?" he called.

"We've found a frog!" shouted Mikhail.

"And they're being mean to it!" Eliza yelled.

Mr Carter had been coming towards us, but he stopped suddenly. "Eliza, put it through the fence," he said, and he headed back to the Sports Leaders' Club, without waiting to see what we did.

The boys muttered and drifted off. Aisha and Eliza kneeled beside me.

"Time for Operation Frog Rescue," I said.

"Princesses at action stations!" said Eliza.

"Ooh, yes," said Aisha. "This is Secret Princess Club business, isn't it?"

"It certainly is," I agreed. "Princess Elisabetta, Princess Araminta – you two stand by, in case he tries to escape."

They nodded. Neither of them seemed very keen to actually pick up the frog though, I noticed. So, rather nervously, I put one hand flat in front of him, then gently nudged him forward with the other. I just managed not to jump as *he* jumped, very suddenly, on to my palm. Aisha squeaked. (And it wasn't even *her* palm.)

I had been afraid that the frog would be

slimy, but he wasn't. He felt warm and light.

I stared into his green eyes. "Hello, Frederick Frog. Do you like your new name?"

I could tell he did by the way his eyes bulged.

Eliza said, "Come on then, Princess Clarinda. You'd better put him though the fence."

I was still staring at the frog. I was getting one of my *feelings*. Slowly, I shook my head.

"But you have to, Chloe," said Aisha. "You heard what Mr Carter said."

"I heard," I said slowly. "But the fact is he doesn't *know*. That we are princesses, I mean. And us being princesses … and this being a frog … don't you see?"

Aisha squeaked suddenly. "Do you mean he's a prince?"

"Of course I do."

"Are you going to kiss him?"

"Well, it's on our list – don't you remember?"

"That's ridiculous," said Eliza. "It's a *frog*. There's loads of them around at this time of year. We get them in our garden all the time."

"Don't you see?" I said again. "We started our own Secret Princess Club and now here is this frog, come from nowhere. There's never been a frog in the school playground before. *Of course* we have to kiss him!"

Aisha whimpered. "I don't want to." Aisha hates touching things that feel strange. When we did our school trip to an aquarium last year she wouldn't even touch the seaweed.

"You won't catch me kissing it!" Eliza said. "I think you're crackers."

I stared at the little creature. I just *knew* that trapped inside was an enchanted prince. I could almost see him transforming in front of me! I was surprised Aisha and Eliza couldn't see it too.

"But it *can't* be a coincidence. Just when I was talking about how we needed a bit of magic. It was *meant* to happen."

"Uh-oh," said Aisha. "I've heard you say things were *meant* to happen before. All it's ever *meant* is trouble."

"This time it's different! Remember our motto: "Act Like A Princess And You Can Be A Princess." And Froggy can be a prince! If you believe hard enough, anything can happen and – hey, what do you lot want?"

Barney and Mikhail were back, and they'd brought some of the other boys with them.

"It was our frog first," said Barney.

"Give it to us, Chlo," said Arthur. "Barney knows about reptiles. He's got a lizard and a snake at home."

"If Barney knew that much, he'd know a frog isn't a reptile," Eliza pointed out. "It's an amphibian."

Everyone started to bicker. Meanwhile, poor Froggy was trembling in my hands. I was sure that inside his froggy chest, his princely heart was beating overtime.

Then Mr Carter arrived. "Now then, what's going on?"

"She's got a frog!" yelled the boys, pointing at me.

"Not … not a real one?" asked Mr Carter in a rather peculiar sort of voice. "I thought I told you to get rid of it, Eliza?"

"Well, yes…" Eliza began.

I wasn't listening. I was looking at poor Froggy. I knew he was waiting for me to release him from the spell. In another moment, Mr Carter would make us put him through the fence and out the playground. It was now or never.

"We *all* have to do it," I hissed at Aisha and Eliza. "It's our Royal Duty!"

I took a deep breath, then raised Froggy to my lips and kissed him gently on his froggy forehead.

"Yuk!" jeered the boys.

Aisha gave a sort of gasp. Then she wrinkled her nose, bent down and gave the frog a quick kiss too. I looked hard at Eliza. "Oh, if I must," she groaned. She leaned forward. But the frog didn't like the look of Eliza. Or maybe he'd had enough kissing. With one giant leap, he was out of my hands and on to Mr Carter's shoulder, where he sat, quivering.

Mr Carter quivered too.

Then he swayed, like a tree in a strong breeze. His knees buckled and he fell sideways into a heap. He'd fainted.

Oops.

Well, we weren't to know Mr Carter had a frog phobia, were we?

Chapter Nine

You will be glad to know that Froggy was fine. He went jumping across the playground and didn't stop until he was through the railings and out on to some grass. Mr Carter went around for the rest of the week with a big sticking plaster on his forehead – otherwise he was the same as usual.

I still wonder what would have happened if Eliza had kissed Froggy too. But I suppose we will never know.

I think it did work some kind of magic. Because we all three felt really good about the Princess Club again. And later Aisha added it to the list in our notebook. It was getting quite long.

Princess Challenges
Baking jam tarts ✓
Learning to ballroom dance
(made a start) 1/2
Making a princess boudoir
(until it broke) 1/2
Helping the sick ✓
Saving a kitten ✓
Kissing a frog 2/3

The following day, I was so busy wondering what the Princess Club should do next that I almost missed Mr Carter's announcement. He said that there was going to be a workshop on our topic that term – which was the Ancient Egyptians.

Everyone was pleased, even when Mr Carter told Barney that no, unfortunately the workshop would not include making mummies – or getting their brains out through their noses with fish hooks.

"Typical," grumbled Barney. "We never get to do anything good."

Aisha, Eliza and I were really excited. We did our special Princess Finger Shake at breaktime.

"It's a shame, though, that we aren't doing a more princess-y bit of history," said Eliza. "Like, maybe Tudor times."

"Yes," I agreed. "Those Tudors wore lovely dresses."

"Even if they did get their heads chopped off," Aisha added.

The workshop took place on Wednesday

in the assembly hall. Eliza, Aisha and I sat together. There was an actor dressed up as a pharaoh, and an actress in an amazing headdress who was supposed to be the Goddess Isis. They told us loads of things about the Nile and pyramids and stuff like that.

Then we made papyrus scrolls and wrote on them.

After that we got to dress up as Ancient Egyptians. Barney was dancing around with a dog's head on, being some kind of god, and Arthur and Mikhail were being Egyptian soldiers.

"And this costume belongs to Cleopatra," said the Goddess Isis (well, the actress pretending to be the Goddess Isis). "Do you all know who she was? She was the last pharaoh of Ancient Egypt."

"How can she be a pharaoh if she's a girl?" asked Mikhail.

"Pharaoh means ruler — but you can think of her as a queen or princess, if you like."

My eyes were feasting on the golden dress. When I heard the word "princess" my hand shot into the air.

"Oh, please, *please* let me be Princess Cleopatra!" I begged.

"No, me," gasped Aisha, waving her hand. "I had my hand up first."

"Actually, I think Chloe's hand went up first," said Eliza.

"Also Chloe is almost the same name as Cleopatra," I said. "Chloe — Cleo. Don't you see — *it's meant to be.*"

The Goddess Isis chose me. I could see from her face that Aisha wasn't pleased.

I paraded around in my wonderful Cleopatra costume. As well as the long, shimmering dress, I wore a belt with a jewelled buckle, a blue-and-gold necklace and a heavy gold bracelet. Best of all, there was a black wig.

"What d'you think?" I asked, posing in my wig. I tried walking like an Egyptian, with my arms at funny angles like in their wall paintings.

Aisha ignored me. Or maybe she didn't hear. (Some of the boys dressed as soldiers had started a bit of a sword fight and the

clatter of wooden swords made a lot of noise.)

"I love it," said Eliza. She whispered to me, "It's a different kind of princess, but just as good as fairytales."

Aisha was trying on a servant girl outfit, but when I suggested she could act out serving me food off a golden platter, she turned her back.

We had to clear up soon after that, and I really, *really* didn't want to take off that golden dress. I kept imagining I really was an Egyptian princess.

"Now, Cleo, get your head out of the clouds," said Mr Carter. "You've already locked yourself into a cupboard – we don't want you locking yourself into a sarcophagus!"

A sarcophagus is what the Ancient Egyptians put their mummies into. The boys laughed, but I didn't care. After all, if I hadn't locked myself in a cupboard that time, we'd never have had the Secret Princess Club.

But when we lined up to go back to class, I found Aisha had already paired up with Fatima. And when I tried to catch her eye and smile, she didn't take any notice.

That night, I told my family that I wanted to change my name to Cleo. (I almost said *Princess* Cleo, but I bit it back just in time.)

"I chose *Chloe* because it's the most beautiful name in the world," said Mum fondly. "It means 'green shoot'. I can't think why you'd want to change it."

"Maybe I don't want to be a green shoot. Anyway I like Cleo."

Dad said I should wait six months, and

if I still wanted to change it, I could.

"But I want to be Cleo *now*."

"Yes, and not long ago you wanted to be Jasmine, and before that it was Willow, and before that – do I remember a Serafina? And before that…"

"This time I won't change my mind."

"Just like you didn't change your mind about ballet – and tap dancing and street dancing."

Arthur remarked, "She wants to be Cleo because she dressed up as Cleopatra today."

I wish he wouldn't interfere!

Dad said to me, "Then you definitely don't want to be a Cleo. I mean, we all know what happened to Cleopatra."

Actually, I didn't. Only I didn't want to say so. Luckily, Arthur asked for me.

"What *did* happen to Cleopatra?"

"She was bitten by an asp and died."

"What's an asp?" I asked. I was imagining some kind of poisonous giant ant. Or maybe a beetle. The Ancient Egyptians were very into beetles. They even made beetle-shaped jewelry.

"It's a snake," said Dad.

"My friend Barney's got a snake," said Arthur. "It lives in a tank and sometimes it gets out and wanders around the house. Can I have one?"

"No," said Mum and Dad in chorus.

"And that goes for you too, Chloe," Mum added.

"I don't want a snake."

"I mean, you're not going to be called Cleo, and that's that."

I reminded her that it was *her* who'd said I could be anything I wanted to be if only I believed it, and I *believed* I was a Cleo, but she wouldn't change her mind.

Chapter Ten

Maybe it was a good thing I couldn't change my name. As I said to Eliza, when we got out our packed lunches next day, even the word "Cleopatra" seemed to turn Aisha into a massive grumpy-chops. Mr Carter had called me "Cleopatra" as a joke when he was handing out our spelling books, and Aisha had scowled like a wicked witch.

Eliza agreed. "It's a shame. I was thinking

we could *all* be Ancient Egyptian princesses. We could wear headdresses and do lots of eye make-up and take baths in milk."

"*Baths in milk?*"

"Yes. Asses' milk. That's what Cleopatra did. I'm not sure what an ass is," Eliza admitted. "Something like a donkey. Or a mule. Maybe we could go to a donkey sanctuary and find out."

"But why would you want to take baths in their milk?"

"It makes your skin silky soft. Didn't you know that Cleopatra was meant to be the most beautiful woman in the world?"

"Really?" (Now I wanted to be Cleopatra more than ever.)

"Yes. And all because she bathed in asses' milk."

I liked the sound of this. "Maybe we could suggest it when we go to Aisha's later?" (The Secret Princess Club was meeting at Aisha's that afternoon.)

"Maybe," said Eliza, through a mouthful of sandwich.

I'd been too busy chatting to remember to eat. Now I took the lid off my lunch box.

"Look at that," I said mournfully. "I've been suggesting all kinds of princess-y lunches to Mum, but she never takes any notice."

Only yesterday I'd written a menu for her in my best handwriting.

Cucumber sandwiches on thinly sliced white bread
Two cherry tomatoes
Five strawberries dusted with icing sugar
Raspberry mousse
Elderflower cordial

And here's what was in my lunch box:

- ♥ *One squashed-looking sausage roll (rather stale)*
- ♥ *An overripe tomato*
- ♥ *A leftover roast potato*
- ♥ *A banana*
- ♥ *A bottle of tap water*

Eliza sighed. "Mine's no better. Hummus on brown bread. And Mum's favourite – carrot sticks."

We shook our heads.

"I mean, we try so hard to train them," I said.

"I know, they're not really worthy to be our parents," Eliza agreed.

"Maybe we should advertise for new ones. *Wanted – caring and queenly mother for a secret princess.*"

We began to giggle.

Aisha came into the room.

"I finished my dinner *ages* ago," she complained, sitting next to us. "I've been

waiting for you all by myself in the playground, and now it's raining."

"We quite often wait for you," Eliza said.

"But there's two of you."

"Well, I'm sorry," said Eliza. "I guess we were chatting."

"You were *laughing*," said Aisha accusingly.

"Eliza's had some really good ideas," I said quickly. "About how we can do princess stuff, just like Cleopatra."

Cleopatra.

Oops.

Aisha glowered. "You should have let *me* be Cleopatra, Chloe. I really wanted to do it. And I look more like Cleopatra than you. She was dark, like me."

"I suppose that's true," I said uncertainly.

"And usually princesses have fair hair. Like Rapunzel or Sleeping Beauty in the school play last year. So there are lots of princesses *you* can be, Chloe."

I was feeling really bad. But Eliza said, "Actually, Fatima was Sleeping Beauty in the play. And she's not fair."

Aisha glowered even harder. She doesn't often get into a mood, but she was in one now.

"Look," I said quickly. "Let's not argue. When we go to your house today, we'll do whatever *you* want to do. And remember — if you believe, and work hard, you can be any kind of princess you want."

Aisha didn't look one hundred per cent convinced.

On the way home, Aisha decided we'd make perfumes, but it turned out her mum needed the kitchen counter to cook Aisha's little brothers' tea.

So we sat and chatted to Aisha's dad who was sitting at the kitchen table eating his breakfast. He'd only just got up, because he'd been working all night driving his taxi.

"I hope none of you girls behave like

some of the people in my taxi when you're older," he said, rolling his eyes at us.

"Why, what were they doing?" asked Eliza nosily. I was curious too. Aisha sighed, as if she had heard it all before.

Mr Akbal shook his head. "Silly things. Sometimes grown-ups behave like little children. They make more noise than those three." He nodded towards Aisha's little brothers, who were throwing Lego at each other on the floor. "And they have worse manners too."

"We try hard to have good manners," said Eliza primly, and we grinned at each other. Manners are an important part of being a princess. And we did remember them – well, most of the time.

"You do have good manners," agreed Mr Akbal. "And that's why I'm glad you two are friends with Aisha. But what game are you all playing together, I wonder? I've noticed Aisha writing a lot in her little book. She says it's a secret."

Aisha said, "Daddy!" We felt embarrassed and he laughed at us. "Ah, well. You girls keep your secrets if you want." He got up to take his plate to the sink.

"Let's go upstairs," Aisha whispered. "Maybe we can make perfumes in the bathroom." But that was no good either, because the sink was full of washing. We went into Aisha's bedroom.

I like Aisha's room. It's tiny, but it's all hers, and it's so neat it's unreal. She even remembers to make her bed each morning, which I never do. Also, she has a dressing table with a pink ruffle round it and a duvet with a pattern of pink roses.

We sat on the floor to talk about what we would do for our next Princess Challenge, while Aisha got ready to make notes in the special club notebook.

"I've got loads of ideas," Eliza began bossily. I could see Aisha frowning.

"Why don't we hear *Aisha's* ideas?" I suggested.

That made Eliza frown at *me*. "But I was speaking first."

"Well…" I said, but at that moment Aisha's mum called her and she went downstairs.

Then I had an idea of my own. "What *I* think is we should choose something from the Princess lists we made at the very beginning," I told Eliza. "They were things we *all* thought of."

"Good idea," Eliza agreed. She reached for the club notebook with the unicorn cover, which Aisha had half-pushed under a cushion. We'd stuck our lists of ideas into the notebook when we'd started the club, but we hadn't looked at them for a while.

Eliza started flicking through the notebook, but then she slowed down and began to read. "I think Aisha's been writing some kind of diary in here."

"Really? Well, we can't read her diary."

"Actually," Eliza said, "it looks more like a story. 'The Diary of Princess Araminta'," she read aloud. "Shall we have a look?"

Now, something inside me was saying that we should NOT read Aisha's diary. Even if it wasn't about her, but only make-believe things about Princess Araminta. So when Eliza said, "After all, she wouldn't have written it in here if it was private because this is the club's notebook," I should have said, "No! Close the notebook!"

But I didn't.

And then Eliza said, "Hey, there's some stuff in here about us!" and instead of saying,

Stop! I said, "Let me see!"

"She's writing about Princess Elisabetta and Princess Clarinda," Eliza went on. "We're all sisters apparently ... wait a minute! She's calling us the Ugly Sisters!"

With that, I leaned over her shoulder and began to read too.

As usual, Princess Elisabetta and Princess Clarinda were being extremely mean and selfish in the run up to the ball, and leaving out their dear sister, the lovely Araminta.

"I'm definitely wearing this pink ball dress," said ugly Elisabetta in a bossy way.

"And I'm wearing this golden one," said Clarinda. She forgot that gold was Araminta's favourite colour. Or maybe she didn't want to remember because she was so selfish.

Poor Princess Araminta! As usual, her bossy sisters had everything their own way and she had to wear a shabby old blue ball dress. Only what her ugly sisters didn't realize was that even in a shabby old dress Araminta looked a hundred times nicer than they did!

"Well," I gasped. And then the bedroom door opened and Aisha was standing there.

"What are you doing? Give me that!" She dived for the notebook.

Eliza held it out of reach. "Ugly Elisabetta!" she said.

"Selfish Clarinda," I said.

Aisha tried to grab the notebook. "You weren't supposed to look!"

"We can see *that*," said Eliza.

"It's just a story." Aisha's lower lip was wobbling. "I was going to tear out that page."

"It's a story that says some very mean things about us," Eliza replied. "Like calling us Ugly Sisters."

"Well, y-you say m-mean things about me. And you leave me out."

"No, we don't," I said.

"Every lunchtime you do!"

"We can't help it if we're packed lunch and you're not." Eliza was looking fierce.

"Today I was waiting and waiting in the playground and you didn't come out for ages and ages."

"Yes, but…"

"And when I wanted to be Cleopatra,

Chloe didn't care how *I* felt. She didn't care at all! And you took her side!" She pointed at Eliza.

"What about *me*?" I demanded. "I wanted to be Cleopatra and you didn't care how *I* felt!"

"I did," said Aisha. "But it was my turn. I had to be the prince in *The Princess and the Pea* – remember? And" – she pointed at Eliza – "she's always taking charge."

"Look," I said, "we didn't mean to leave you out, and Eliza can't help being a bit bossy..."

"What do you mean, *bossy*?" demanded Eliza. "At least I was never silly enough to get shut in a cupboard!"

And suddenly we were all glaring at each other. Eliza, with her hands on her hips. Aisha, with her lower lip wobbling and her eyes welling with tears. And me, beetroot

red (I knew I was because my face felt so hot).

Our Secret Princess Club was in big trouble.

In fact, it was beginning to look like there wasn't even going to be a Secret Princess Club.

Chapter Eleven

At school next day we ignored each other.

When we had to line up for the bell, we got into different parts of the line.

When Mr Carter said, "Get into groups, everyone, we're going to make a pyramid," we got into different groups.

When breaktime came, Aisha went off with Fatima and Amy to play handball. Eliza went to Library Club.

I sat by myself in the playground. Or

that's what I did until Arthur threw a football at me. I kicked it back, and ended up joining in the game.

But after school I felt really sad.

Of course, Aisha and I had fallen out before. You can't be best friends with someone for as long as we have and not fall out. It had never felt like this, though. At least, I didn't think it had.

Aisha had never written mean stories about me, for example. *Ugly, selfish Princess Clarinda!* How could she?

Of course, now I came to think of it, I'd once written a story that included *her*. It was called *The Adventures of the Amazing Chloe*, and Aisha had been the not-so-amazing helper, who got to watch every time Amazing Chloe did something else amazing and wonderful. And she hadn't been very bright either – Amazing Chloe was always having to explain things to her.

Aisha hadn't liked that story much, I seemed to remember.

And she hadn't even *seen* my poem. The one I wrote when I was really, really mad with Aisha that time she missed my birthday because she had to go to her cousins' party instead. The one that began,

Aisha is a real old meanie
And she looks like a frog wearing a bikini.

I'd ripped that poem into little pieces but — I had to admit — it had made me feel a lot better writing it.

After all, Aisha hadn't meant me to read her story.

On the other hand, I reminded myself, she had written it in the Secret Princess Club Notebook.

Even so, maybe we shouldn't have read it without asking her.

"What do you think, Hammy?" I asked.
Hammy opened one eye and looked at
me (he probably wouldn't even have done
that, except that I'd just poked him with

my finger) and went back to sleep. I poked
him again, and he heaved himself awake
and went to run on his wheel.

My thoughts were going round and

round too, just like Hammy on his wheel, and getting nowhere.

I couldn't talk to Aisha because I was mad at her. I couldn't talk to Eliza because she was mad at *me*. Besides, if I did, Aisha would probably think we were ganging up. And I couldn't talk to anyone else without mentioning the Secret Princess Club. And the most important rule of the club was that it was *secret*.

While I was thinking all this, the doorbell rang. I went to see who it was (I was half-hoping it might be Aisha) but it was Barney. He had come for a sleepover.

I was annoyed.

"That's not fair," I told my parents. "When *I* had a sleepover, *Arthur* got to have one too. So if he's having a sleepover, so should I!"

Nobody took any notice.

I went back to my room and did some work on Hammy's royal palace. It didn't go very well. "Without the Secret Princess Club, I'll never finish it," I told Hammy gloomily, as one of the turrets fell off. "I need Aisha's help. I'm not as good at making things as her."

Then the boys began crashing around making the most terrible noise.

STAMP! STAMP! THUMP! THUMP! BANG! BANG!

They even started roaring! I stuck my fingers in my ears. It wouldn't be so bad, I thought, if only Aisha and Eliza were here. We could spy on the boys, or attack them with pillows. Being just one was no fun at all.

Things didn't get any better after tea. Arthur and Barney were allowed to choose a film to watch. "Because after all, there are two of them, Chloe," said Dad. And they chose a scary one about dinosaurs, and I don't like those kinds of films because they give me nightmares.

So I went back to my room.

If only I were a *real* princess, I thought. Princesses didn't have fallings-out with their friends. I bet they always chose which film to watch too.

If I were Princess Cleopatra, *I* would be the boss. I would have jewels and servants and a throne.

I wouldn't have two other princesses trying to take charge, either. I would be Top Princess.

And why shouldn't I be? Just because the others weren't here – that didn't matter. I didn't need them! I could be a princess *all by myself*.

I sneaked into my parents' bedroom. I

remembered what happened last time I borrowed Mum's clothes, so this time I was very considerate. I chose Mum's oldest blue kimono, and a gold scarf I know she doesn't really like for a belt.

I still had my gold sandals from the summer holidays. They were a bit tight, but I managed to squeeze my feet into them.

It was difficult to know what to do about my fair hair. I thought about dipping it in black ink – only I didn't have any black ink. So I found another scarf and wrapped it round my head. After all, lots of Ancient Egyptians wore headdresses – we'd seen pictures at school. On top of the scarf, I pinned one of Mum's necklaces.

I still didn't look enough like Cleopatra. But I knew how to fix that.

I sat down at Mum's dressing table and got

going with her make-up. Pictures of Egyptian queens and princesses always show them with amazing colours around their eyes. With the help of Mum's eyeshadow, I soon had amazing colours around *my* eyes, too.

Finally, I attached Mum's biggest, dangliest earrings to my ears with sticky tape.

I paraded up and down in front of the long mirror. I looked great.

Now, what else did Cleopatra do?

Of course – she bathed in asses' milk.

I stood in front of the mirror and waved a regal hand. "Go fill my bath with sweet milk of asses, oh humble slave girl!"

"Yes, Highness, it shall be done," replied the humble slave girl. (I was playing the part of the humble slave girl too.)

I crept downstairs and past the living room, where I could hear the dinosaurs roaring, and Arthur and Barney arguing.

("That's a stegosaurus." "No, it's not. It's a triceratops.")

There was lots of milk in the fridge, but somehow when I'd taken it upstairs and poured it into the bath, it didn't look that

much. So I took all the cartons of UHT milk from the cupboard under the stairs where Mum and Dad store them.

I wanted to *wallow* in milk. I wanted to have it swooshing around my neck and shoulders, giving me beautiful, soft skin, just like Cleopatra. I wanted to paddle around like a happy hippo. But every time I poured in a carton of milk, it was as if it disappeared. It felt as if the bath wasn't filling up at all.

"I'm a princess – I'm not bathing in a puddle!" I told my humble slave girl. "I shall do some magic. It will be a spell for MORE MILK!"

I needed some kind of potion for the magic, so I fetched Mum's bottle of Chanel No 5. I only meant to use a few drops, as it's a *very* expensive perfume, but my hand joggled.

Oops.

"Multiply, oh milk!" I commanded. "Become like the River Nile!"

I shut my eyes tight.

I could feel a kind of buzzing around me. I was sure the magic was working. I wondered what would happen if it worked too well, and the milk *did* turn into the Nile. I could picture it overflowing the sides of the bath and cascading down the stairs.

I opened my eyes quickly. To my relief, the milk was still in the bath. More disappointingly, it didn't seem to have multiplied much. Or even at all.

"Oh, well," I said. "I'll have to make do."

I locked the bathroom door then stuck one toe into the bath, just to see what it felt like.

It was *cold*. I don't like cold baths (I know that because when our boiler broke down there was no hot water for a whole week). I wondered if Cleopatra had liked cold baths? Perhaps she had, because Egypt was so hot? Or had she heated the milk first?

Maybe, I thought, I could *imagine* the milk was warm ... and that I was lying in a marble tub ... and being fanned with ostrich feathers. I began to picture the scene. Instead of a wilting fern in a pot, there was a palm tree, and instead of Mum's shower cap, there was a snake hanging from the tap...

Wait. There really was a snake hanging from the tap!

I gasped.

Don't panic, Chloe, I told myself. *There has to be an explanation.*

Like, for example:

1) I'd fallen asleep and was dreaming.

I pinched myself hard but I didn't wake up.

2) I was imagining I was Cleopatra, and because Cleopatra had been bitten by a snake, I had got carried away and imagined a snake.

But it really was there.

3) It was a toy snake belonging to Arthur that I had forgotten.

This seemed quite a good explanation until the snake lifted its head and looked at me out of its little yellow eyes. It hissed.

I gave a huge, piercing shriek.

Chapter Twelve

There was the sound of thundering feet on the stairs. Then shouts from the landing.

"Chloe! What's going on?"

"Open the door!"

I couldn't open the door. I had a big bath towel in both hands, and I was holding it up so the snake couldn't get me. If it came any closer I was going to throw the towel over it. That way it couldn't bite me.

"Chloe!" my parents yelled again.

"Snake!" I shrieked – and other stuff too, like, "Help!"

CRASH!

The door burst open. Dad had kicked it down! Mum was there too, and Arthur and—

"That's *my* snake!" Barney yelled, grabbing it.

"What's it doing here?" Dad demanded.

"I brought her with me," said Barney. "She's my pet. And she doesn't bite," he added.

Dad looked as if *he* might bite. After he had told Barney off about the snake, Mum said, "What *are* you wearing, Chloe? And why is the bath full of *milk*?"

Arthur said, "Maybe she's making a giant rice pudding."

"Why would I do that?" I demanded. "I don't even like *normal*-sized rice pudding."

"So what *are* you doing with all that milk?"

"I'm bathing in it, of course."

"Run that past me again," said Dad.

"I'm bathing in asses' milk. Well, it's not asses' milk, 'cos we don't have any asses, and I don't see why asses' milk should be that different anyway, because it's all milk, and it makes your skin silky soft. Only then this asp, I mean, snake, came along so I got distracted."

Everyone goggled at me.

Then Arthur gave a yell. "Chloe's being Cleopatra!"

"*Ahhhh*," said Mum and Dad together, as they finally understood. As if I hadn't explained it perfectly well already!

Unfortunately, *understanding* didn't make them exactly *understanding,* if you see what I mean. They were really cross and there was a big Telling Off. They blamed me and my imagination, as usual, and seemed to think it was my fault Dad had broken the lock on the bathroom door.

There were two good things, though. One was that Mum hadn't noticed about the Chanel No 5. (Phew!) The other was that Barney and Arthur were in worse trouble than me. Mum and Dad said it was "utterly irresponsible" of Barney to bring his pet snake and let it loose like that. They called Barney's parents to come and fetch him and his snake home.

I managed not to fret too much over the weekend, but on Monday morning all my worries came flooding back. Would Eliza and Aisha ever speak to me again? And what would happen to the Secret Princess Club?

I was so anxious that I had to talk to somebody. So while we were getting ready for school, I told Arthur I'd fallen out with Aisha and Eliza.

"So, what do you think?" I asked.

"What do I think about what?" He was rummaging in his school bag.

"What do you think about how I can make it up with them, of course?"

"Oh. I don't know."

"Well, how do *you* make it up when *you* fall out with your friends? Do you talk to them? Write them a letter? Apologize?"

Arthur considered. "We usually just thump each other. That sorts it out."

I sighed. "I'm not going to thump Aisha because she'd be really upset. And I'm not going to thump Eliza because she knows karate!"

Arthur dropped his bag and a notebook fell out. I picked it up. It had a dinosaur on the cover.

"Hey, give that me!"

"I'm just trying to help!" I said as he snatched it away and went stomping off down the hall.

Honestly, I thought, I might as well have asked Hammy for advice. Twin brothers really weren't much use. I went on worrying about what to do all through the journey to school, and Assembly, and the start of our first lesson – which was Mental Maths. Until a scrunched-up ball of paper hit me on the arm.

It was a note.

At first I hoped it might be from Aisha, asking to make up, but it wasn't.

Ha ha! Yore Secret is Out. Everyone WiLL Know about the Poopy Prinsess CLub!

My heart gave a thud. When I looked up, Barney was smirking at me.

He knew! He didn't just know about

Cleopatra – he had guessed about the Secret Princess Club too. He must have overheard me talking about it to Hammy.

It seemed doubly unfair that everyone was going to find out our secret, now we didn't even really have a Secret Princess Club.

I scrunched up my eyes and made myself think, really *think*. And not about Mental Maths. I was making a *plan*.

The trouble was, I didn't think I could do it all by myself. But then again, maybe I didn't have to.

One thing was for sure – there was no time to lose.

The whole future of the Secret Princess Club was at stake!

Chapter Thirteen

It was lunchtime. And because it was Monday, it was our class's turn for Computer Club.

I put my head round the door of the Resources Centre and looked around. There was no sign of Miss Hammond. There weren't many kids, either. It was a really sunny day, and everyone else was in the playground, not peering at a computer screen.

Except, that is, for Arthur, Mikhail and Barney.

They were working really hard on something. They didn't notice me, creeping up behind them.

"Right, what about Rule Two?" Arthur said. He had his notebook open beside him.

"Maybe that should be about our special names," said Mikhail. "We should always use them."

I was so close. I could have tweaked Arthur's ear. Or pulled Barney's hair. Or yelled "Surprise!" But I didn't. I looked over their shoulders at the computer screen.

Ah ha! Just as I'd suspected.

"Having fun?" I asked in a loud voice. Then I grabbed Arthur's notebook.

"Hey! Give that back!"

"No way."

"Ooh! It's the Poopy Princess!" yelled Barney. "Princess Chloe! We know all about your secret club!"

"Yeah, and I know all about *yours*, Barney," I replied. "Or should I say —" I glanced down at the notebook — "Mr Diplodocus?"

"Actually *I'm* Mr Diplodocus," said Mikhail. "He's Mr Triceratops."

"Shh!" hissed Arthur. He turned to me. "You don't know anything!"

"Yes I do," I told him. "I can be a detective too. I've heard you lot a million times, pretending to be dinosaurs. Clumping about! Pretending to roar! Watching dinosaur films. Then I saw what was written on your notebook this morning. And it's written *there*, too."

I pointed at the computer screen.

The Secret Dinosaur Club
Rules: Every Dinosaur Must Have a
Speshul Roar. . .

"And that's not how you spell special," I added.

For a moment the boys looked really glum. Then they got mad. They stood up. They narrowed their eyes. They started to walk towards me...

They were snorting, like angry dinosaurs.

And there were three of them and only one of me.

"HAAAAAAAI CHAAA!"

Eliza burst into the room. She was wearing her karate kit!

She did a complicated kick in the air. Then some chopping movements with her hands. Then some quick punches. She lifted

her foot and took aim at Barney...

"Get off!" yelled Barney trying to hide behind Mikhail.

"Tell her to stop," Arthur said to me. "Before she breaks something and we get banned from Computer Club forever!"

"We'll leave you alone," I replied. "But only if you promise never, ever to breathe a word about the Secret Princess Club."

"Otherwise I'll kick your butt!" put in Eliza.

"And we'll tell *everyone* about Mr Diplodocus, Mr Triceratops and..." I looked questioningly at Arthur.

"Mr Stegosaurus," he muttered.

"I'd have thought one of you'd want to be Mr T-rex," said Eliza.

"We all did," Arthur said. "That was the problem."

Aisha came rushing into the room. "Miss

Hammond is coming!" she gasped. (Aisha had taken on the job of keeping Miss Hammond out of the way.)

I looked at the boys. "Quick! Do we have a deal or not?"

They nodded.

"Promise?"

"Promise," they muttered.

We all sat down and bent over our keyboards as Miss Hammond entered the room. But secretly Aisha, Eliza and I grinned at each other.

"Full marks," I whispered, "to Team Princess!"

We didn't have a chance to talk much until going-home time. Then we all stood in the playground and smiled shyly at each other.

"That was great work, wasn't it?"

"We showed them!"

"You should have seen their faces when Eliza came bursting in."

"Eliza, you were just like Princess Fiona in *Shrek*!"

"Do you mean I look like an ogre?"

"No, I mean you're really good at karate! Will you teach us some moves?"

"Aisha, you did a great job with Miss Hammond."

"Chloe, you were so clever guessing their secret."

I blushed. "Oh, well, it wasn't that hard."

"If it wasn't for you, Barney Big Mouth would have told everyone."

"It if wasn't for *all* of us, you mean."

I was almost hopping with excitement. I was *so* glad my plan had worked. I'd been really, really nervous when I'd gone up to

Eliza and Aisha at breaktime and asked for their help. I'd been afraid they'd say no. But when they'd heard what Barney was up to, they'd agreed immediately.

We hadn't had a lot of time to discuss anything else, though. And now we had sorted out the boys, I wasn't sure whether they might not go back to how they were before.

"Does this mean," I asked hopefully, "that we're still the Secret Princess Club? That we're still friends?"

"Of course!" said Eliza.

"Definitely," said Aisha.

I said to Aisha, "I'm *really* sorry about Cleopatra. And I shouldn't have left you out."

Aisha said, "I'm sorry I wrote that diary."

Eliza said, "I'm sorry I read it. That was my fault. I persuaded Chloe."

"I shouldn't have been persuaded."

"I shouldn't have been bossy."

Suddenly none of it mattered any more.

We beamed at each other.

The Secret Princess Club was back!

Chapter Fourteen

"Can you fix my tiara?" asked Aisha, gesturing at her head.

"How about mine – is it straight?" asked Eliza anxiously.

I fixed Aisha's tiara more securely with a hairgrip. It had red stones in it, like rubies. Then I turned to Eliza and made sure her emerald tiara was straight, instead of dangling over one ear.

Aisha giggled. "Do you think all princesses do this?"

"Of course they do," I said.

We were at my house. We were having an extra-special meeting of the Secret Princess Club. We'd decided we'd done so many Princess Challenges that we really were princesses now, and that we deserved to have a coronation.

"I just wish *my* tiara hadn't got squashed," I said sadly.

"Well, actually…"

Aisha brought out a box with a ribbon round it, and held it towards me.

"This is for you."

I gave a joyful squeak as I looked inside. Aisha had made me a new tiara with gold swirls and blue stones, like sapphires. "It's even nicer than the old one!" Then Aisha and Eliza made sure that *my* tiara was on straight too.

"Almost time for tea," said Aisha.

We were going to have a special
coronation banquet. We'd helped make it,
and we were really looking forward to it.
There were finger sandwiches and mini-
pizzas and crackers with cream cheese.
There were mini bhajis and samosas
(from Aisha's mum) and lots of chopped
vegetables and mini bagels (Eliza's mother
sent those). There were tiny jellies with
layers of different colours, and bite-sized

chocolate mini rolls, and little cakes with royal icing (of course) and sugar butterflies and glacé cherries on top. The table was decorated with fairy lights and there were lovely napkins with unicorns that we'd bought with our own money.

"I can't wait," I said.

"My stomach's rumbling," Eliza agreed.

"First let's look at our list of Princess Challenges," said Aisha. We got out the notebook, and read through everything we had done.

Princess Challenges

Baking princess tarts ✓
Learning to ballroom dance
(well, made a start) 1/2
Making a princess boudoir
(until it collapsed) 1/2

Helping the sick ✓
Saving a kitten ✓
Kissing a frog ✓
Being Cleopatra ✓
Wearing tiaras ✓
Doing karate (like Princess
Fiona) ✓

"I suppose not everything worked out perfectly," said Aisha.

"But we did our best," I added.

"And we definitely deserve a coronation," Eliza finished. "Especially *you*, Chloe."

I was really surprised. Aisha was nodding.

"The thing is," Eliza went on, "there wouldn't be a Secret Princess Club if you hadn't thought of it."

"And then saved it," Aisha added.

I knew I was going beetroot red again. But I didn't care.

"You two are the bestest friends ever! And do you know what? It's no good being a princess without friends."

"Let's have a hug!" said Aisha.

So we did. Even Eliza, who isn't a huggy sort of person.

It was time for the banquet. Before going downstairs we curtseyed to each other and did our special Princess Finger Shake.

"Long live the Secret Princess Club!" we yelled. "Princesses for ever!"

The Secret Princess Club Notebook

Members: ♥ Princess Araminta
           ♥ Princess Clarinda
           ♥ Princess Elisabetta

We declare our Secret Princess Club
has been a big success. We have
behaved with grace, wisdom and
maturity (whatever Barney Big Mouth
and the boys say. Also their Dinosaur
Club just copied ours and was stupid).

We are elegant and kind.
We understand about Ancient Worlds.
We have done kindnesses and learned
to dance and defeated snakes and
become karate champions.

Most of all, we have stuck together
and had fun!

Long Live the Princesses!

The Princesses Will Be
Friends Forever

Signed,

Their Bestest Highnesses
Araminta
Clarinda
Elisabetta

Which Princess are you?

What colour jewel would you have in your tiara?

a) Blue
b) Green
c) Red

What's your bedroom like?

a) Messy but full of your favourite things
b) Pretty and colourful – with some secrets hidden away
c) Neat and tidy

Choose a fun activity:

a) Playing make-believe
b) Martial arts
c) Arts and crafts

What are you most like?

a) Dreamy and imaginative
b) Down to earth
c) Kind but a bit shy

Who is your favourite princess?

a) Sleeping Beauty – you wish you had a four-poster bed
b) Elsa – you want to go on a snowy adventure
c) Cinderella – you want to ride in a horse and carriage

What do you want to be when you grow up?

a) An actress
b) A doctor
c) An artist

Mostly A's: Princess Clarinda!

You are Princess Clarinda! Just like Chloe, you have a wonderful imagination and love to make up fun games with your friends. You never get bored as there's always an adventure to be had.

Mostly B's: Princess Elisabetta!

You are Princess Elisabetta! You are calm and organized and never forget to do your homework. Like Eliza, you love learning new things, and you probably sing or

play a musical instrument too.

Mostly C's: Princess Araminta!

 You are Princess Araminta! You are kind and patient, even with your brothers and sisters. You love making things and drawing pictures, and you are a wonderful friend.

Start Your Own Club!

Why not start your own club, just like Chloe, Aisha and Eliza? It's a great way to spend time with your friends and try out new hobbies.

Here are some tips for starting your club, but all you really need is some imagination!

♥ **Decide what your club is going to be about.** Do you want to start a secret detective club where you solve mysteries? Maybe you want a dance club where you and your friends can get together and try out some routines? A pirate club, a book club, an astronaut club, or even a dinosaur club like Arthur's – anything is possible!

♥ **Invite some members.** Who do you want to join your club? Chloe asked her two friends, Aisha and Eliza, but you could have any number of members. They don't have to be friends either – you could include family members, pets, or even your teddies!

♥ **Next you'll need a name for your club**. You could include your own name, like Chloe, or if it's a secret club, you might just want to use initials. SHARP! could stand for Secret Hero Amazing Rescue Posse!

♥ **Think of a secret handshake or password** for your club members to use. Maybe you could have a competition to choose the best one?

♥ **You might want to choose special names** for the club members, just like Chloe and her friends chose to be "Clarinda", "Elisabetta" and "Araminta".

♥ **Start a club notebook.** Write down all your club secrets, ideas and discoveries so you don't forget them. You could also make to-do lists and tick them off, just like they do in the story.

♥ **Find the perfect meeting place.** This could be your bedroom, underneath a favourite tree or a special spot in the playground.

♥ **Get creative!** Like Aisha in the story, you and the other club members could make fun badges. Or, if you want to invite new members to join, why not make posters (only do this if your club isn't secret though!)?

♥ **Have fun!** Don't worry about making too many rules for your club – you can make these up as you go along. The important thing is to have lots and lots of fun, whether you're being a princess or a pirate!

Princess Jam Tarts

Why don't you have a go at making Princess Jam Tarts, just like Chloe, Aisha and Eliza do in the story!

Ingredients

For pastry: 85g unsalted butter

170g self-raising flour
(or you can buy ready-made short crust pastry. Then you can go straight to Step 3!)

Jam – raspberry, strawberry, apricot – whichever is your favourite!

You will also need a jam tart or cupcake tray and a grown-up to help you with the oven.

1) Preheat oven to 200C/400F/Gas 6.

2) Rub the butter and flour together in a

bowl until it looks like crumbs. Gradually mix in a few tablespoons of water to make a dough.

3) Roll out the dough – scatter some flour underneath it so it doesn't stick. Use a pastry cutter or cup to cut out about 15 circles.

4) Grease the tray with a little butter or margarine.

5) Put each circle of pastry into each hole of the tray. Add a teaspoon of jam to each. (Don't add too much!) If you like, make little crowns from the pastry scraps and pop them on top.

6) Ask a grown-up to put the tray in the oven. Cook for 30 minutes, or until the pastry is pale brown (check after 20 minutes).

P.s - Make sure they don't burn!

Emma Barnes has always been a bookworm. She was born and raised in Edinburgh, where she spent hours making up stories for her younger sister. Emma's first writing success came when she won a short story competition – the prize was a pair of shoes. Emma wears the shoes for school visits, where she loves to spark children's imaginations and create a passion for writing and stories. Emma now lives in Yorkshire with her husband, daughter and Rocky the dog.

www.emmabarnes.info